STAR TREK® III
THE SEARCH FOR SPOCK
STORYBOOK

BY LAWRENCE WEINBERG
BASED ON THE SCREENPLAY WRITTEN BY HARVE BENNETT

Little Simon
Published by Simon & Schuster, Inc., New York

STAR TREK® III: THE SEARCH FOR SPOCK
STORYBOOK
Lawrence Weinberg
Photographs courtesy of Paramount Pictures
Corporation

Designed by Stan S. Drate

Manufactured in the United States of America

10 9 8 7 6 5 4 3 2 1

Like a proud but wounded lion, the great starship *Enterprise* limped slowly homeward through space. Her sides were battered, some of her instruments didn't work, and she could only move on impulse power. But these were the marks of her triumph. Her torpedoes had destroyed the wily outlaw Khan and preserved the secret of Genesis; the formula that had already turned one dead planet into a bursting Garden of Eden was safely stored in her memory banks. At last, in just over two hours, she would be sighting Earth.

A hero's welcome most probably awaited her commander and crew, yet standing upon her bridgedeck, Admiral James T. Kirk couldn't care less. Spock, who had roamed the universe with him for twenty years, had given his life to save the crew and ship. He was gone forever, leaving behind an emptiness that all the medals in the galaxy couldn't fill.

For a second time, Kirk gazed down at the decoded message he held in his hand.

Science team orbiting Genesis planet reports detection of pho-ton tube on surface believed to contain Spock's remains. Appar-ent lack of damage due to atmospheric cushion effect. Investi-gation of unusual planetary changes continues.

Jim's thoughts went back to the funeral and the dark moment he had ordered the casket dropped from the ship. "So you landed softly, old friend," he whispered. "I'm glad."

All at once he felt very weary and turned away from the officers at the controls. "Mr. Sulu, take over. I'm going below to my quarters."

He entered the waiting elevator and started to descend, but before he reached his level, the doors opened and the ship's doctor, "Bones" McCoy, entered.

Jim studied him closely. McCoy was unshaven, wild-eyed, and looked as if he had been sleeping in his clothes for weeks. The doctor's peculiar behavior had been going on for some time now, and Jim was worried. The physician was growing worse, instead of snapping out of it.

"Where are we headed, Admiral?" McCoy asked suddenly.

This too was strange. McCoy knew the destination perfectly well. "Earth," Kirk answered, his voice betraying his concern.

"Then," snapped the doctor as if he were accusing Kirk of a crime, "we're going in the *wrong* direction!"

"I don't understand, Bones. What's wrong with you? This is me! Jim. Your friend."

McCoy's look grew odder still. *"And I have been . . . and always shall be . . . yours."*

A chill went up Jim's spine. Those were Spock's dying words! Had Bones gone mad?

If so, McCoy's *madness* seemed to grow deeper, for now it was Spock's own voice that rose in torment from the doctor's throat. "You left me, Jim. You sent me down to Genesis. Why did you do that?"

"What are you saying!" Jim gasped in horrified disbelief. "Bones, why are you doing this!"

McCoy blinked and shook his head as if he were trying to rid himself of some strange influence. "I don't know," he said at last in his own, but trembling, voice. "I just . . . Jim, I can't get it out of my head that it was wrong to leave Spock back there."

"But he's *dead!*"

The elevator stopped and McCoy stepped off. "Dead like a being of our planet?" the doctor asked, turning to face him once more with that same strange-eyed look. "Or like a Vulcan?"

The door of the elevator closed, leaving Jim more alone than he had ever felt before.

In another spacecraft very far away, Jim Kirk's own son, David Marcus, stood behind Lieutenant Saavik staring at the science station monitor.

"Animal life forms on Genesis!" he exclaimed. "Are you sure? I can't believe it. When my mother and I designed this project, we only made it possible for plants to grow down there!"

"That may be," replied Saavik with the self-control possessed by even half-Vulcans. "But there are life energy readings in the area where the fallen casket is located."

In great excitement, David turned to Captain Estaban, the officer in charge of the small Federation research vessel. "Beam us to the surface immediately!"

Estaban shook his head. "The rules don't permit that when there's any possibility of danger."

"The danger, Captain," David fairly shouted at this man who seemed more concerned about rules and regulations than science, "is that we won't find out what it is that is down there. Or *who!*"

The captain reluctantly gave in against his better judgment. "I just hope that we're not buying a lot of trouble that I'll wind up being responsible for."

"You're a prince among men!" David sang out enthusiastically, as he and Saavik collected their gear and stepped onto the disk in the transporter room. In a column of shimmering, dancing light, they disintegrated . . . and began the journey from which one of them would never, ever return.

In the endless darkness between two galaxies, a ship with no running lights glided slowly toward a secret rendezvous. Its captain, seated at the control panel, shook his head and turned to his only passenger.

"Don't matter how much you pay me, lady. I can't afford to be carrying around a Klingon spy for the rest of my life. The scanner don't show up nothing. There ain't another vessel out here in this quadrant."

"Put me on the hailing frequency," the half-veiled woman answered, stepping toward the communication panel. "Commander Kruge, my noble lord," she called. "It is I, Valkris. I have obtained the Federation data and am ready to transmit."

Out of the black nothingness of space, a voice as hard as metal traveled back. "You have done well. Stand by as we de-cloak."

The captain looked up suddenly at his screen to discover it was no longer empty; a hawklike skeleton had snapped into being and began to slowly fill out . . . into a deadly Klingon Bird of Prey!

"It . . . It . . . was invisible!" the dumbfounded man stammered.

"Transmit data!" ordered the Klingon Commander.

The woman inserted a small disk into the console. The top secret report she had intercepted on its way from the U.S.S. *Enterprise* to Federation Headquarters was fed at ultra-speed to the waiting warship.

"Transmission completed," Valkis said. She paused, then added softly, "I have seen the data."

"That is unfortunate," replied the Commander's voice, with just the barest trace of hesitation. "You know what I must do."

"I understand," she answered calmly. "Success, my noble lord, and my love!"

"What's going on?" muttered the captain of the smuggling ship. The Bird of Prey had dipped her wings as if preparing for a dive. "When do we get paid off?"

In a voice that already sounded as cold as death, the woman answered. "Now."

From the claws of the birdlike ship two blazing phaser beams shot forth. Instantly, the attacked spacecraft burst into exploding flames. Seconds later, she and all who were inside her had ceased to exist.

Aboard the Klingon vessel, the warlord Kruge spoke to his officers. "Any race who has Genesis, the power to make new worlds for new populations to live on, has the power to take over the universe! If the

Federation uses it for their own, the Klingon Empire will become as nothing, and our race will die out. We must have the knowledge for ourselves alone! This data only tells us *what* they did, not how they did it. Alter course. We make for the new planet!"

Unaware of the danger faced by his son and Lieutenant Saavik on Genesis, Admiral Kirk gave the final orders for entering the huge spacedock orbiting Earth. The big gates of Entrance Fifteen slid open, and the battered starship slipped at last from the endlessness of space toward its home berth.

There were many ships of the fleet docked inside the gigantic structure, but the crew of the *Enterprise* had eyes for only one. A gleaming Superstarship sat at an impressively spotlighted mooring, flaunting state-of-the-art in every sleek curve.

"Will you look at the size of her!" Commander Uhuru exclaimed. "I've never seen anything like it."

"You're looking," said Jim, "at the newest and the best! *Excelsior*, ready for trial runs."

"Best!" Scotty, the ship's engineer, snorted. "Maybe she'll beat us for speed with her fancy new transwarp drive, but she'll never have the heart and soul of *this* old girl!" He patted the *Enterprise*'s control panel lovingly.

Jim shared in this feeling and he smiled.

All at once, the spell was broken.

"This is impossible!" cried Chekov, who was on duty at the science station. "I sealed that room myself. Admiral, I'm getting an energy reading from Mr. Spock's quarters. There's life form in there!"

"All right, calm yourself, Mr. Chekov. I'll have a look," said Jim, resting a reassuring hand on the officer's shoulder.

As soon as he was away from his crew, Jim lost all of his own calmness. Rushing down C deck, he arrived at Spock's door and found the seal ripped away, as if by some powerful force. Cautiously he slipped into the darkened room. Before he could reach for a light, a voice called out to him from the blackness, making his hand freeze on the switch. It was Spock's, and it sounded as if it had come from the grave.

"Jim . . . help me. . . . Take me back to Vulcan . . . up the steps . . . of Mount Seleya . . . through the Hall of Ancient Thought. . . ."

"It can't be," Jim muttered, visibly shaken. "Spock?" Forgetting all about the light, or perhaps even wary of what he might see, Jim stepped uncertainly toward the shadowy form in the darkness. Suddenly, the speaker bolted for the door.

"Wait!" Jim lunged, and his body made contact with something that was not phantom, but flesh and bone. Whoever—or whatever—it was, struggled with great power to break free, but Jim would not let go. They toppled to the floor, grappling with each other. Then all at once, as if a force from within had suddenly relinquished its hold on the body, the fight

eaching for a switch, Jim threw on the light and saw . . . the limp
g form of Dr. McCoy!

God!" thought Jim. "He *is* mad."

, the doctor's eyes began to focus. He seemed to be coming
mself. Desperately, Jim took him by the shoulders and
s friend's face for a flicker of recognition. "Bones, listen to me.
u are not Spock! Your home is here, on Earth! Do you understand?"

McCoy nodded.

"Then tell me that. *Say it to me!*"

McCoy opened his mouth. It was Spock's voice that came out of it.
"Remember!" he shouted. "Remember!" And with a shudder, the doctor
collapsed.

Just then, it was announced over the ship's intercom that the
commander of the entire Federation Starfleet was coming aboard for
inspection; his timing couldn't have been worse. "Uhuru!" Jim ordered,
"get medical help down here at once!" Jim stayed close to his friend's
side until the medics arrived, then rose, straightened himself, and went to
the deck. For the time being, Jim was determined to say nothing about
this to the Admiral.

The meeting with the Starfleet commander went off very well, at first.
He and Jim had great affection for each other, and Admiral Morrow was
full of praise for a job much more than well done. Except for Mr. Scott,
there would be shore leave for all. The Chief Engineer, the Admiral
cheerfully announced, was to go aboard the new superstarship *Excelsior*
as captain of engineers.

Scotty was not happy about it. "Begging the Admiral's pardon, but I'm needed here to refit the *Enterprise.*"

The Starfleet Commander chose this moment to "lower the boom." There would be no refitting, he told them all. "This ship is a generation old. Time for her to retire in glory. And time for you, Jim, to get back to your shore desk."

Kirk's mind was in a turmoil. McCoy may have been raving, but those words—Spock's words—still echoed in his mind. "Jim . . . help me. . . . Take me back to Vulcan." And then, too, his son was still out there in the Genesis sector. The boy was brilliant, but impulsive.

"Sir," Jim said quickly. "At least let us return, to finish what we began."

The admiral was firm. "Out of the question. The whole experiment has caused a scientific uproar. Until the Federation Council decides what to do, no one is to go there or even speak about it. No one. Those are strictest orders. Do I make myself clear?"

"Very clear," Jim answered with resignation.

What the Admiral didn't know was that his determined colleague had anything but given up.

Lieutenant Saavik gazed in puzzlement around her. This new world had been created only a short time before, yet she and Dr. Marcus had materialized in the middle of a forest where trees were already soaring overhead.

How could such a growth take place so soon?" she asked, and kneeled to the ground. "We'll need soil samples for a study of the aging process going on here."

But David was impatient. "Not now; later! We're here to investigate life forms, remember? Tricorder's leading us that way." He set off at a quick lope. "Come on!"

Crossing a creek, they climbed a little hill and began to weave their way through a thick patch of subtropical vines and ferns leading them back into woods again.

Captain Estaban's distant voice crackled from the tiny communicator in Saavik's hand. "*Grissom* to landing party. Our readings from here show you approaching radioactive area."

"Thank you, Captain," she replied, "but our own readings indicate it to be well below danger level."

"Still, advise caution."

Paying no attention, David hurried ahead to a clearing in the woods. When Saavik caught up, she found him staring at a metal object not twenty feet away. It was the photon tube: Spock's coffin.

"There is your life reading, Lieutenant," he said in a disappointed tone. The ground around the tube was littered with a seething mass of wormy little creatures. "The dead haven't by some miracle come alive, and Genesis doesn't produce any animal forms. Their ancestors must have been microbes on the tube's surface. We shot them here ourselves from the *Enterprise*."

Ancestors? Saavik thought. But it would have taken billions of years of evolution for microbes to have developed into *these*! "How could it have happened so quickly?" she wondered aloud.

"Don't know," said David, struggling to overcome his feelings of disgust as he waded through the worms to the casket.

"Well?" asked Saavik. She had hung back only because she did not want to see what the slimy things must have done to the body of the Vulcan she had admired so much during his lifetime. "What do you see?"

"Only this." He lifted out a long length of black cloth.

"Spock's funeral robe," Saavik affirmed, sadness momentarily clouding her Vulcan features.

"I don't get it," said David in a hushed tone. "He's . . . gone."

So completely astonished were the two young scientists that they hardly noticed the gentle rumbling of the ground beneath their feet. It was only when a distant and eerie howl rose from somewhere on the other side of the forest that they realized how little they knew about this human-made planet called Genesis.

As he stood by the window of his city apartment gazing up at the night sky, Jim Kirk was troubled. "Something's going on out there I should know about," he told himself. "I can feel it. Yet here I am, like a shipwrecked sailor, stranded on the shore of a deserted island."

His restless thoughts were interrupted by the gentle sound of the door chime. "Enter," he called.

A tall and almost ghostlike figure swept into the room, covered from head to foot in a dark Vulcan robe. In every way—size, manner—it was Spock. The figure stopped before him and drew back the hood.

"Sarek!"

Spock's father, the planet Vulcan's ambassador to Earth, wasted no words. "You were my son's closest friend, the last to be with him. Yet you deprived him of his future."

Jim felt he must have heard him wrong. "But Sarek, he was dead."

"His body, yes. But his Katra—his living spirit—was given to you. You were the keeper of his essence until it could enter the Hall of Ancient Thought, until it could leave you to become united with the Eternal Wisdom of our race."

"I . . . I don't understand."

Sarek stared at him searchingly. "Did not my son ask you to carry his soulless body to Mount Seleya so that the sacred ceremony could be performed?"

"No! Sarek, please tell me—"

Sarek interrupted the Admiral with a raised hand. "I must have access to your thoughts. Will you permit me this?" he asked solemnly.

"Of course," Kirk answered.

The Vulcan drew close and positioned his hands on the Admiral's temples. Both men closed their eyes.

"My son spoke to you of friendship," Sarek said quietly.

"Yes," Kirk affirmed softly, distantly, as though from out of a trance.

"He told you not to grieve. . . ."

"Yes. The needs of the many. . . ."

Kirk and Sarek relived Spock's final moments in this fashion, until as last Sarek removed his hands, and the mind meld was broken. He laid a gentle hand on Kirk's shoulder while the Admiral recovered from the experience.

At last, the Vulcan spoke. "Then my son—everything he knew and became—is lost. When I return home emptyhanded, many shall mourn."

Kirk well understood Sarek's intention now. "To communicate his thoughts, Spock would have had to touch me, but that wasn't possible this time. He was in the ship's radiation room, Ambassador. We were separated by a transparent wall."

Sarek turned to leave, but Kirk felt compelled to stop him. "Wait! Please!" Jim cried. "If so much was at stake, surely Spock would have found a way!" All at once he thought of McCoy. If Bones had received the mind meld without realizing it, wouldn't that explain his strange behavior? Bones' confusion of himself with Spock?

But had they been together just before Spock went to his certain death in the radiation room? Did Spock actually have the opportunity to make the contact? The visual recording of what had happened that day would surely show it. And Jim had brought the black box containing all the necessary data down with him.

Minutes later, he and Sarek sat side by side in a tiny electronic studio watching a replay of the last moments of Spock's life. They saw the Vulcan scientist heading for the damaged engine. Saw McCoy trying to head him off in a desperate attempt to stop Spock from destroying his life. Cleverly, Spock tricked him into looking the other way, then sent the doctor reeling into unconsciousness with a nerve pinch. Then, as McCoy fell to the deck, Spock bent over him, placed an open hand on McCoy's temple, and said one word: "Remember."

So *that* was the cause of all McCoy's suffering! This was no bout with "nervous exhaustion" as the doctors here on Earth had called it; and all the pills, shots, and bed rest prescribed would be no use at all to Bones.

"You must bring my son's body and Dr. McCoy to Mount Seleya," said Sarek. "Only there can both of their spirits find peace."

"I have no ship."

"You must get one."

"It is out of bounds for anyone to go to Genesis."

"And therefore?"

"Therefore," Jim told himself, "I shall go anyway."

With that same thought in mind, though he did not understand the reason for it, McCoy rose from his bed, dressed, and left his apartment. Arriving early for his appointment at the Quasar Bar and Grill, he waited impatiently for someone he knew only by name.

A very strange-looking fellow, an alien from a distant planetary system, approached after studying him for a while. "You seek I," he muttered in a low, growling voice. "Available ship stand by. You name place, I name money."

"Genesis," McCoy answered quickly. "How much?"

"Genesis planet forbidden. Not can do."

"I told you I would pay!" cried McCoy, becoming more agitated by the second.

"Not shout. Not business," said the stranger, preparing to rise from his chair.

"Yes, business!" bellowed McCoy, seizing the fellow by the collar and yanking him down.

"Could I offer you a ride home, Dr. McCoy?" The man laid a gentle hand on the doctor's arm.

"How do you know who I am?" Bones barked at him.

"Federation security, sir."

"Leave me alone!" he exploded, leaping up from his chair so suddenly that he accidentally knocked into a waitress, causing her to collide with a group of people nearby. In the confusion, the stranger was

blamed for it and someone took a swing at him. This was McCoy's chance to get away—or so he thought, but the agent grabbed him.

All at once it occurred to McCoy to use Spock's Vulcan nerve pinch. He tried, but the effect was not the one he had anticipated. The security man simply stared at McCoy, then quietly said, "Come along, Doctor. You're going to get a nice, long rest."

There was, however, no rest for David Marcus and Lieutenant Saavik as they followed wherever the voice of the elusive, mysterious life form led. They had left forest country long behind, only to find themselves trudging through the cactus and scrub brush of a broiling desert. Whenever the tricorder failed them, they searched for tracks or waited for the cry that rose in the distance each time the ground shook beneath their feet.

"Whatever is making that sound," David muttered as he wiped the perspiration from his face, "is running away from us. And we're not doing a good job of catching up."

"Look ahead," said Saavik, pointing to a far-off hill. "It's covered with snow. I don't understand all of these sudden changes in climate and the condition of the land. How can all this—?"

Captain Estaban's voice broke in over the lieutenant's communicator. "*Grissom* to Saavik. I have to warn you that we are reading a severe and unnatural age curve on the planet. Those quakes are indications that Genesis is leaping wildly from one stage of its development to another. I'm concerned about your safety."

"*Grissom*, your message received. Will advise. Out." She turned to David. "Do you have an explanation?"

At that moment the ground gave another jolt, and once more the howling cry of a thing in pain filled the air.

"Later!" David replied with typical impatience. "Let's go."

It was a long trek to the high ground of the cold country. By the time they reached it and started to climb, a light snow was falling in flurries around them. At first they had no trouble seeing, but as they went along, the wind grew stronger and the snowfall heavier, and they found themselves in the teeth of a swirling, blinding storm.

"Can't make anything out," Saavik called over the roar of the wind.

"Yeah, but listen to the tricorder; it's going wild! We're near. We're near." All at once, he fell silent. His straining eyes stared into the falling wall of snow. Something had moved just ahead. Moved and disappeared. "Look! Did you see it?"

"I'm not sure, but I think so." Saavik drew her phaser from its holster. Stepping carefully now in the direction the phantom had vanished, she signaled for David to turn off the tricorder for fear that its noisy beeping might alarm the creature.

Low and muffled by the wind, there came a soft, frightened sob. The Vulcan lieutenant and the scientist from Earth found their life form not ten feet away from where they stood.

"*It's a child!*" Saavik whispered, lowering her phaser.

A wild and whimpering boy lay in the snow where he had fallen, clutching his bruised leg and staring at them in terror. While David tried to make some sense of this, Saavik knelt beside the child and reached out to him.

Cringing with fear, the boy, who could not have been older than eight or nine, jerked back. Saavik tried again, moving slowly. This time, he allowed her to touch him. Very gently, her hand traveled up his face to his straggly hair and parted it. The sharp points of his ears became visible. There was now no mistaking the fact that this child . . . was a Vulcan!

"Incredible!" David whispered in awe. "The Genesis wave must have . . . His cells must have been regenerated . . . reformed . . . like a new birth! *This is Spock!*"

Quietly, so as not to alarm the boy, Saavik opened her communicator and relayed the news to the ship. "Captain, may I suggest we beam him aboard immediately?"

"Uh, yes," the dumbfounded Estaban replied hesitantly, "but I think I should advise Starfleet first and get instructions."

"Sir," said Saavik, with all the patience she could muster, "we are experiencing quakes here. They're growing strong. There is absolutely no danger of radioactive contamination from the boy. I'm sure Starfleet would approve."

"Just the same, let's do it by the book, Lieutenant. Stand by."

Aboard the *Grissom,* Captain Estaban turned to his Chief Officer, who was already trying to make contact with headquarters. "What's the problem?"

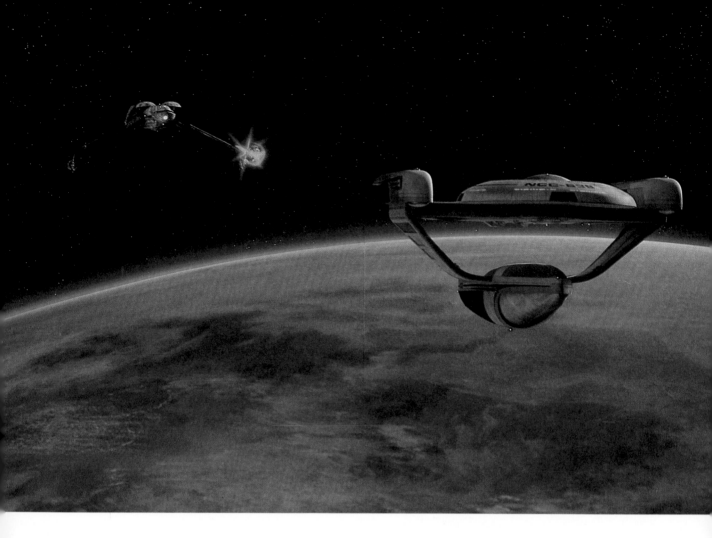

"Can't get through, sir. Something's jamming our transmission. An energy surge from aft quarter."

"Put it on the screen." The monitor lit up. Estaban peered at a field of stars and shook his head. "There's nothing. Just a slight shimmering over there."

But out of this "nothing" there suddenly appeared a Klingon Bird of Prey! "Oh my God!" the captain cried. "Red alert! Raise the shield!"

His order came too late to ward off the deadly photon torpedo that was streaking toward them even as he shouted the command.

Down on Genesis, Saavik tried once more to find out what was going on. "We're under attack!" screamed Estaban over the communicator. There was a roar, then silence.

David stared at the lieutenant as she turned to him with Vulcan calmness and matter-of-factly said, "It would seem that an enemy has destroyed the *Grissom*."

They were marooned together on this heaving, trembling planet, and Saavik felt that it was time David told her the truth about Genesis. Why was it experiencing these quakes? Why did the planet seem to be growing older so fast? How could Spock, who had only been regenerated by the Genesis wave weeks before, have already reached boyhood? There was something very wrong, and she insisted on an answer.

At last, David admitted the truth. "I . . . I used protomatter in the matrix."

"Protomatter!" she shouted, showing her human side for a moment. "But every decent scientist in the galaxy has said it's too unpredictable to use—too dangerous!"

"I know! I know! I should never have done it! But I just wanted to make things happen a little faster. I didn't want to wait twenty years to see how Genesis would work out."

At that moment, the ground gave a powerful jolt. As if something had wrenched inside the child himself, he too cried out, twisting in pain.

David Marcus watched Saavik wrap her arms around the boy and thought, "This crazy planet I invented has given Spock new life, but what else has it done to him? And what will it do to us all?"

For the first time since the brilliant young scientist had been a small child himself, he felt absolutely helpless.

The Klingon warlord was furious. He had given strict orders to cripple the scientific research vessel, not destroy it. The chief gunner paid for his mistake without protest, but Kruge felt no better after he had blasted the man into oblivion. "I wanted prisoners!" he stormed, still waving his phaser.

Torg, his chief officer, dared to speak. "My lord, there are life signs on the planet. Perhaps the very scientists we seek. . . ."

"We shall see," grunted Kruge. And as if it spoke for his master, the hideous pet beast he cradled in his arms opened his jaws and snarled.

When the famous Admiral James T. Kirk stalked into the prison where police were holding Dr. McCoy, asking to see his junior officer, the officials could hardly say no.

"If you had come tomorrow, you wouldn't have found him here," declared the guard who led him through the locked gate and down the corridor. "We're just about to haul him off to the funny farm."

"Yes, the poor fellow's nutty as a fruitcake," Jim pleasantly agreed.

A few minutes later, the two friends were racing down the same corridor, Jim having left the guard where he had decked him, sleeping peacefully on the cellroom floor. "You okay, Bones?" Kirk hurriedly asked as they fled.

"Yeah! This medicine you gave me is great stuff, but knowing what's bothering me is even better. Right, Spock, old buddy?" McCoy replied, and both men smiled at his cryptic reference to the Vulcan.

Reaching the entrance gate, Jim used the electronic key he had taken off the fallen guard, and the gate swung open. Another guard, a towering fellow, blocked their way, but not for long. A hand expertly sliced down from behind in a martial chop; the guard dropped like a crashing tree.

"Dependable as ever, Mr. Sulu, but didn't you hit him a trifle hard?"

"He called me Tiny. This way, Admiral. Hurry!"

Jim quickly sent a coded message over his communicator. "Unit Two, this is One. The *Kobiashi Maru* has set sail for the promised land. Acknowledge!"

"Message acknowledged," replied Chekov, seated at his old station on the *Enterprise.* No sooner did he sign off than Scotty, fresh from his new job on the *Excelsior,* stepped onto the bridge.

"The Admiral believes in short-order miracles," he said, slapping his hands together. "So let's do one and get some life into the old girl!"

While Scotty and Chekov were still working furiously into the night on the starship's battered warp drive, Commander Uhuru sat behind the desk of a sleepy Earthside transporter station.

"What I don't get," complained the bored young lieutenant who worked beside her, "is why a space veteran like you would ask for a nowhere job like this. Nothing ever happens here. No surprises. No adventure!" Just then, he looked up to see three men swiftly enter.

"Good evening, Commander. Everything ready?"

"Come into my parlor, Admiral."

"Wait a minute!" protested the lieutenant, watching the men sweep right by him to the transporter pods. "We can't allow this! First we have to see destination orders and—"

"You wanted adventure?" Uhuru pointed her phaser at him. "How's this? Back up into that closet!" When he was safely tucked away, she turned to the others. "Good luck on your mission. I'll go ahead to Vulcan and meet you there later."

She threw the switch and activated the beam; the two men dissolved in a shimmer of atomic particles, their destination the *Enterprise,* hundreds of miles above the Earth.

As soon as he materialized aboard ship, Jim stepped onto the bridge. "Stations, everyone."

The crew flew to their posts, knowing that at any second they could be discovered.

"Clear all moorings," he ordered. "Engage auto systems." Everything in him longed to pull away from the spacedock with all the speed the *Enterprise* could muster, but that would have to wait until the giant doors of the rotating port had been cleared—doors that were still locked shut. "One-quarter impulse power."

Slowly, the starship slipped away from the long dock. "One minute to spacedoors," Mr. Sulu announced.

McCoy was edgy. "You just going to *walk* through them?"

Before Jim could answer, Chekov looked up from the communications panel to give the worst possible news. "Sir, Starfleet Commander on emergency channel. He orders you to surrender the vessel."

"Continue on course." Jim needed no one to tell him that *Excelsior,* the sleeping giant, would be wide awake now, a yellow alert blasting captain and crew into a frenzy of action.

"Admiral!" Sulu reported not ten seconds later. *"Excelsior* is following."

"I know. How far are we from the spacedoors?"

"Thirty seconds, Admiral. *Excelsior* is gaining."

"Steady. Steady." He turned to his chief engineer. "All set, Mr. Scott?"

"Sir?"

"Open the *doors,* Mr. Scott."

"Working on it, sir." His fingers raced across the electronic keyboard in front of him.

"Admiral! *Excelsior* is closing fast!"

"So are we," thought Jim, for the *Enterprise's* nose was rapidly bearing down upon the still-locked gates.

With a great heave, the gates slowly began to part. But there was no time to wait for them to open fully. Even as the *Enterprise* edged through the narrow opening, its commander thundered, "Warp speed!"

"Aye, sir!" replied Sulu. In an exploding blur of movement, the starship hurtled into open space.

Standing on the bridge of the superstarship *Excelsior,* Captain Styles studied his monitor, and grinned. "No way are you getting away from me, Kirk. When this baby opens up, you'll think you were standing still." He turned to his first officer. "Prepare for warp speed. Stand by to go straight through it to transwarp!"

"Warp and transwarp at your command, sir," came the split-second reply.

"Execute!"

With a surge of power that no machine ever built before could match, the huge spaceship burst forward—then bounced!

"What the devil is going on!" roared the astonished man while the brand-new pride of the fleet coughed, wheezed, and shook itself in space like a wet puppy. "Where is my chief engineer!"

His chief engineer was standing amidst Jim Kirk's smiling crew, holding up a microchip so small one almost had to squint to see it. "Took it out of her main transwarp computer drive."

"You're as good as your word, Mr. Scott. And now, Mr. Sulu, if you please, best speed to Genesis."

The planet groaned and rumbled. The shuddering ground shook the forest as Kruge and his armed search party made their way through the trees, following the life form readings on his Klingon tricorder.

As they entered the grove where Spock's empty casket lay, his soldiers suddenly drew back before a mass of long, slithering serpents. Kruge was made of stronger stuff. A look of contempt crossed the warlord's face, and he strode forward. With a swipe of his bare hand, he snatched up the most powerful looking serpent of them all.

It was a challenge to the death, and the snake met it with alarming ferocity. Lashing out with its tail, the serpent curled itself around the Klingon's throat, wound tightly, and pressed. Kruge's soldiers watched in growing horror as the last gasp of air was forced from their leader. The bones of his neck, bending inward, seemed about to crack. But the warlord, who was as coldblooded as any serpent in the universe, studied his chosen combatant. With one motion, he found its jugular and pressed, concentrating all of his strength there. The writhing creature sprang open like a child's jack-in-the-box, stiffened, and fell away.

"Nothing of importance here," Kruge reported through his communicator to the hovering Bird of Prey. "Am resuming search."

In their hideout up in the mountains, Saavik bent over the suffering Spock. It was almost impossible to believe that under her very eyes he had turned from a young boy into a youth thirteen or fourteen years of age.

"Sleep," she whispered to him in Vulcan, though he seemed unable to learn even the simplest words she had been trying to teach him. He understood the kindness of her touch, but that was all. It was, she thought, as if he had no thinking mind, only instincts. She rose and went out of the cave and found David lost in thought.

"The planet is aging fast," he said. "In spurts."

Saavik nodded. "And Spock along with it, they're joined together. Each new shock is an agony for him, and it's getting worse."

David nodded. "The pressure is building up in the planet's core. If we don't get out of here pretty soon, we'll all be goners."

"How long?"

"Days, maybe hours." He glanced down at his activated tricorder. "Whoever's coming after us is getting closer."

"I'll see what I can find out."

"No, you stay with him. He trusts you." Borrowing her phaser, he stepped out into the night.

Saavik wondered if she should have let him go; she was concerned about David's state of mind. Besides, she was the one with military

training. She thought of overtaking him, but there was a sudden quake, a jolt so hard she fell to the ground. From behind her came a cry of unbearable pain. Staggering to her feet, Saavik started for the cave. Another shock sent her reeling backwards. At last she burst into the opening. The young Spock lay twisting on the ground like a thing gone mad. The tremors were coming thick and fast now, and each new one drove him wilder with agony.

"It will pass," she whispered fervently, as she knelt beside him. "It will pass. It will pass."

The night wore on, but David did not return. In her exhaustion, Saavik could no longer remain on guard. She fell asleep shortly before dawn—and did not hear the Klingon soldiers enter the cave.

The Klingons dragged Saavik and the young Spock out of the cave and flung them at the feet of their warlord; David stood nearby between two menacing Klingon guards. "I'm sorry I couldn't stop them, Lieutenant! But maybe *you* could reason with him. He's after Genesis, like Khan was, and I can't make him see that it's worthless!"

"My lord," said Saavik, with all the logic she could pull together, "consider the situation. The planet is surging from one age to another. Who can live on it? It is useful to no one. In hours it will burst apart. The Genesis experiment is a failure."

"Destructive power such as this," Kruge scowled, "and you call it a *failure?* I will have the secret from you or—"

"Sir!" his sergeant interrupted. "Report from bridge. Federation starship approaching."

Instantly the prisoners were forgotten and Kruge snatched the communicator from the soldier's hand. "Status?" he demanded with a roar.

"We are cloaking ship now, my lord," came the reply from space.

"Bring me up!" He threw the communicator back to his sergeant and, in a shimmer of light, vanished.

Chekov blinked and took another look at the scanner on the science panel of the *Enterprise.* Had he or had he not, just for the barest fraction of a second, seen a bluish flash on the space field? He reported his concern to the admiral.

"Could be the *Grissom,*" Jim replied. "Let's try reaching her again."

Standing on the bridge of the Bird of Prey, Kruge listened to the starship commander's attempts to contact the destroyed science vessel. "Admiral Kirk calling Captain Estaban or Lieutenant Saavik. Come in!"

The warlord cocked an eye toward his second in command. "Enemy closing on impulse power, sir. Range, five thousand kellicams."

"They are unaware of us," muttered the Klingon warlord. "Good. Stand by to transfer all necessary energy from cloaking device to weapons!"

Receiving no reply from the science ship, Jim grew worried. "Give me a short-range scan, Mr. Chekov, and put it on the screen; let's have a close-up look."

The spacefield surrounding the planet Genesis appeared upon the monitor. "There!" said Jim, pointing to a tiny shimmering area off near a corner of the screen. "Opinion, Mr. Sulu?"

"It seems to be coming closer, Admiral."

"Identify."

"I think it's an energy form of some kind, sir."

"Enough energy to hide a ship, would you say?"

"You mean a cloaking device, sir?"

"Red alert!"

"My lord," reported Commander Kruge's officer, "we are within range. One thousand kellicams."

"Wait, wait. She is much stronger than our vessel. I want a perfect target. Stand by to de-cloak."

"Jim," said McCoy anxiously, "they are almost on top of us. Why don't we fire?"

The Admiral's eyes remained fixed on the screen as he spoke. "Because we need a better look at it. If my guess is right, they'll have to de-cloak before they can fire. Mr. Scott! Two photon torpedoes at the ready. Stand by for my signal. I think it's going to show up just about . . ."

"My lord," called the eager Klingon gunner. "Five hundred kellicams."

"Very well. Stand by torpedoes. De-cloak!"

" . . . Now!" cried Jim as the Bird of Prey broke into view. "FIRE!"

The *Enterprise* rocketed two torpedoes. Eating up space in gulps, they slammed into the Klingon warship before she could launch her own. The stricken Bird of Prey lurched backwards, while disorder and destruction spread throughout her interior.

Staggering among the wreckage, Commander Kruge struggled to save his ship. "Emergency power to the thrusters! We must stabilize!"

Moments later, an officer reported, "The ship's responding, my lord. She moves slowly, but we have control."

"Good! Lateral thrust. Stand by weapons." He turned his gaze upon the screen. "They haven't raised their shields. There is still a chance!"

"Scotty!" Jim called anxiously. "Why aren't the shields going up?"

"There was no time back in spacedock for everything, sir. Never thought we were going into combat."

"Admiral, torpedoes coming at us!"

"Sulu! Evade!"

"No time, sir!"

The first explosion caught the *Enterprise* square amidships, sending flames shooting off in every direction. The second landed near the bridge itself. Crew members went flying; consoles sizzled with electrical fire. Except for the raging fires, the entire ship from stem to stern was plunged into deep blackness.

"Emergency power!" Jim roared, pulling himself to his feet. Dimly, only dimly, lights went on again. "Mr. Scott, stand by to return fire."

"We can't, sir. And we can't go anywhere, either; they've knocked out the automation center!"

Jim's glance darted to Mr. Sulu, who was getting no response at all from the ship's helm. "So," the Admiral muttered to himself, "we're a sitting duck. Unless . . ."

The image of a human being flashed upon the viewscreen of the Klingon ship. "This is Admiral James T. Kirk of the Federation Starship *Enterprise*."

"So!" Kruge grunted to himself. "The commander of the Genesis experiment himself."

"Your ship is badly damaged," Jim went on. "I give you no more than two minutes to surrender. Do so or we will destroy you."

Kruge was too cunning to be fooled, he sensed that Kirk's ship was in worse trouble than his own. Besides, he had hostages. "Admiral, on the planet below I have three prisoners from your science team. It is you who must surrender immediately or I shall execute them all."

"How . . . how do I know you have them?"

Kruge's orders were quickly relayed to the Klingon sergeant left behind on Genesis. A moment later, Jim heard a familiar voice coming in. "Admiral—"

"Saavik! Is—" His throat tightened and he began again. "Is David with you?"

"Yes. Along with a Vulcan of your acquaintance."

Jim could not believe what he heard. "I . . . I don't understand. Are you saying he's *alive?*"

"Yes, exactly. Though in body only."

"In body only," Jim repeated to himself softly.

"Hello, sir," It was David's voice breaking in.

Jim's heart leaped. In the short time since he had learned he had a son, the young man had grown to mean so much to him. And now his life was in terrible danger! "David, I'll do everything I can—"

"This is all so ridiculous!" David blurted. "This planet is about to destroy itself. Genesis doesn't work! It's no use to anyone! I can't believe they would kill us for it!"

Kruge cut him off. "Your young friend is quite wrong about what is of use to us and what we will do to get it. I mean what I say. And to prove it, I am ordering one of the prisoners killed immediately."

"Wait! Wait!" Jim Kirk cried frantically. "Give me a chance!"

But Kruge had already sent the order down to the planet below.

On the planet below, the Klingon sergeant put away his communicator. He drew a dagger from its sheath and stepped toward the prisoners, eyeing them one by one. The choice was his, and he intended to play the role of executioner to the hilt.

He stopped before the ill and mindless Spock. The boy was nothing, he thought; a wasted kill. He next turned his gaze on the man. The man babbled; he was no soldier! But the woman . . . the woman seemed so self-controlled and unafraid. An inner voice prompted him: "Her." This one, he told himself, was worthy of death delivered by a Klingon dagger. The dagger rose in his hand and hovered in the air, poised to strike.

"No!" David screamed and, breaking free of his captors, leaped at the man. But the glinting blade was already on its deadly descent, coming down, down. There was a thud as David Marcus crashed into Saavik; she fell away, and in his chest, David took the plunging blade.

Aboard the *Enterprise,* Jim heard the cry of death and his mind went blank. "Admiral"—it was Saavik on the communicator—"David is gone."

Jim felt just as if the same dagger had been thrust through his own breast. *Oh, my son, my son,* his brain now whispered, and he howled aloud. "Klingon dog! *You've killed my son!*"

Kruge was unmoved. "There are two more prisoners yet to go. Surrender your vessel now!"

In spite of his grief, the Admiral forced himself to think. His own life meant nothing to him now, but he had to find a way to save Saavik and Spock. "All right! All right!" he cried. "Give me a minute to inform my crew."

In the Klingon code of honor there was no room for mercy, but the warlord respected a gallant enemy. "I grant you *two* minutes. No more."

Hollow-eyed, Jim turned to his men. "I swear to you we're not finished yet. Mr. Chekov, you will give your computer orders to self-destruct according to sequence. Mr. Scott will do the same with his. And I"—he rose suddenly from his commander's chair—"will scuttle my ship."

Feverishly, the crew rushed through their tasks. "Kirk!" the voice of the Klingon leader barked out. "Your time ends. Report!"

"Everyone to the transporter room," Jim ordered. "Hurry!"

"Kirk!"

Jim flipped the communicator switch. "Commander, Klingon vessel. Your forces may come over. We are energizing transporter beam . . . now." Setting the controls in motion, Jim leaped to the pad beside his men. "Let's go." Nothing happened. "What's wrong, Mr. Scott?"

"Power is weak, sir, but it's building."

"It better!"

With a sudden upsurge, the beam came on, and all who were on the *Enterprise* vanished. A bare half-second later, the Klingon boarding party materialized upon the same spot.

"Round up everyone," Lieutenant Torg commanded.

As his soldiers carefully searched the great starship, they paid no attention to the voice of the main computer softly counting down in a language they did not understand. "Twenty-two. Twenty-one. Twenty."

Lieutenant Torg contacted the Bird of Prey from the captured ship. "My lord, it appears to be deserted."

"What is that sound in the background?"

"A computer, sir. It appears to be running the bridge."

"Let me hear it more clearly."

The officer placed his communicator close to the computer's speaker. "Six. Five. Four."

"It's a trap!" Kruge bellowed. "Get out!"

Torg turned to his troops. "To the beam!"

"One," said the computer, softly, and the U.S.S. *Enterprise* blew apart.

From where they had materialized on Genesis, the little band looked up. Together they watched the *Enterprise* plunge like a comet through the twilight sky. They were witnessing more than the death of a starship; for twenty years, the legendary *Enterprise* had shared their destiny. Ship and crew had been inseparable partners in the ongoing mission to explore strange new worlds . . . to seek out new life forms . . . new civilizations . . . to boldly go where no man or woman had gone before.

Heartsick, they turned away, speaking not a word as they set out to find Spock, Saavik, and the body of Admiral Kirk's son.

The two soldiers Kruge had left behind to guard the prisoners were alarmed. Trees and boulders trembled around them; lightning flashed; the ground seethed beneath their feet as if an enormous volcano

were about to erupt; and, above the loud crashings and rumblings of the planet, the wild shrieks of the Vulcan tore at their nerves.

Deciding to at least put an end to the screaming, one of them rushed toward Spock. "Don't touch him!" Saavik cried, throwing herself between them. Savagely, the Klingon pushed her aside and drew his phaser, but Spock's thrashing head movements and the sight of his face, stretching in all directions like a mound of clay, made the soldier freeze in his steps.

"What is it?" demanded his sergeant, pulling out his own weapon.

"Don't move!" Jim roared, bursting into the clearing behind them. Both Klingons whirled on him at once. Firing off two stun blasts, Jim dropped them in their tracks. He started to run, but the sight of his fallen son, half covered by leaves, brought him to a stop.

"David," he whispered, kneeling beside the body. All the aching grief he had been holding back returned in a rush. "My dearest son, my dearest son. To thee no star be dark. Both heaven and earth, friend to thee forever."

Saavik's question to Dr. McCoy nearby reminded him of the still-living. "Why has Spock stopped screaming so suddenly?"

"He's slipped into a coma."

"What else, Bones?" Jim asked, rising.

"He's growing older at a furious rate. Everything is speeding up."

"And his mind?"

Bones' reply half-sounded like something Spock would have said himself. "It would seem, Admiral, that *I've* got all his marbles."

"My God, isn't there any way to stop it?"

Saavik came forward. "Only if we get him off this planet right away. His aging is part of what's going on around us."

"Our ship is gone," Scotty told her gently.

"Yes, *our* ship," Jim said quickly. "But not *theirs.*" He snapped on the communicator. "Kirk to Klingon commander. Sorry about your crew, old boy, but that's life. I am in your camp on the planet. Now about the Genesis secret you want so much: I have it, only you'll have to beam us up to get it. What is your answer?"

Perhaps because of the incredible thundering of the sky and the shuddering ground underfoot, the Admiral received no answer except static. What now? he asked himself. What could he possibly come up with?

"Drop all weapons!" commanded a voice behind him. Jim turned. It was Kruge! "Over there," ordered the Klingon warlord, motioning with his phaser. "All but Kirk, and the one who is dying."

The little band moved off as they were told, leaving Jim and the unconscious Spock. Kruge lifted a communicator to his lips, calling out in his own language. "Lieutenant Maltz! Prisoners are at beam coordinates. Activate!" In a shimmer of light, Jim's crew was gone.

"Well, here we are," Jim told the Klingon pleasantly. "Just the three of us, and the raging forces of nature. This place is about to go, you know."

Kruge was not disturbed. "Genesis. I want it."

"You fool! Look around you. The planet is destroying itself!"

"Yes! Exhilarating, isn't it!"

"If we don't help each other, we'll all die here!"

"Perfect! That's the way it shall be. Give me Genesis!"

"Beam us all aboard first and then we'll talk about it."

"Here!" The warlord aimed his phaser. "NOW!"

As Kruge made ready to fire, the boulder on which he was standing suddenly heaved upward, throwing him off balance. This was Jim's chance. With a flying leap, he toppled his huge enemy; they fell together among the quaking rocks.

But Jim's initial advantage of speed and surprise was soon over-come; the Klingon was much more powerfully built. Kruge threw him off and rose, his hands and feet landing one murderous blow after another. Though he fought back with everything he had, Jim was reeling with exhaustion and pain. Then, with one tremendous smash to the jaw, the warlord sent him sprawling backwards to the ground. Taking advantage of his momentary victory, the Klingon went for his weapon.

Jim had to stop him now or die! Desperately lashing out with his feet, he caught Kruge by the legs. A quick roll, and the Klingon tripped and went down. Jim pounced. Once more the warlord's strength began to tell, but Jim held on, and the two foes, grappling with each other, tumbled down a long slope leading to a precipice. Jim caught a glimpse of it and, with a tremendous push, he broke free; the huge Klingon could not stop himself in time. Suddenly, he went over.

Jim rushed to the edge, sensing that somehow the warlord was not finished yet. He was right. With fingers barely clinging to a jutting rock just below, Commander Kruge dangled over a great, endless abyss.

"I'll pull you up," Jim called, "if you get us off this planet."

"Give me Genesis!"

"Do you think I keep it all in my head? No! Genesis is gone with my ship. Now give me your hand—and live!"

"I have failed," said the Klingon, in a rush of self-hatred. "But I'll take you with me!" With a devilish surge of strength, he sprang upward to grab at his enemy's leg.

"Not a chance!" Jim lashed out, and the warlord, slipping back, fell down, down, down with a vanishing cry. . . .

Losing no time, Kirk ran back to the place where the Vulcan still lay in his coma. The changes that had taken place in only the last few minutes shocked Jim. The boyish face had given way to the mature face of the Spock he knew! Throwing his friend over his shoulder, he snapped on his communicator and barked in Klingon, "Maltz! Activate beam!"

Then he waited, hoping with all his heart that his imitation of the warlord's voice had worked.

Lieutenant Maltz, the only Klingon left aboard the Bird of Prey, was standing guard over his prisoners when he heard the order. Something peculiar about the way his commander had sounded made him hesitate at the transporter controls. "Distortion," the lieutenant assured himself. The eruptions below were changing the sound of his master's voice. He turned the dial.

By the time he realized his mistake, the Klingon officer was facing the barrel of an enemy phaser. It was a moment of great dishonor. "Kill me!" he demanded, almost pleadingly.

"Sorry," declared Jim. "Not my style. Now help us out of here!"

But Maltz was too stunned. For a few precious moments Jim's crew racked their brains, trying to manipulate the unfamiliar controls. There was every need to rush; the spaceship was hovering between Genesis and its sun. When the collapsing planet fell out of orbit, it would be coming straight at them!

"If I read this right, Admiral," Sulu said at last, "we have full power."

"Go!"

The Bird of Prey turned slowly, gathering speed. And then it happened. A starburst below changed Genesis into a seething, onrushing ball of fire. "Warp speed!" commanded Jim, and the ship rocketed away to the safety of outer space.

Onward they raced toward Vulcan. Surely, Jim told his crew, a way could be found on Mount Seleya to make Spock whole again; Saavik, the half-Vulcan, informed him otherwise. "What you suggest—returning his spirit to his body—is most unusual. The elders may not choose to try it."

"And if they don't?"

"Then McCoy will give up Spock's Katra to the Hall of Ancient Thought, and the body will remain as it is."

"But that's, that's horrible! A living death! Listen, I want you to send a message ahead to his father, Ambassador Sarek. Explain the situation to him."

There had been much preparation for their arrival. By the time Jim set the vessel down near the foot of the sacred Vulcan mountain, Commander Uhuru was there to meet them. She pointed to the temple atop the hill. "Sarek is waiting above."

A dense crowd of Vulcans were already assembled. They had come in the night to pay homage to the great space scientist Spock. Jim and his crew carried the motionless body past the flaming torches lining their path on either side.

As they neared the huge temple, six robed priestesses stepped forward to take the body from them. Jim's eyes fastened searchingly upon Sarek. "Follow and wait," was all the Vulcan said, then he turned and entered behind his son.

The High Priestess summoned the old man to her and spoke. "The body of thy son breathes still. What is thy wish?"

"I ask for Fal-Tor-Pan, the refusion."

"Only in legends have we learned of this. Your request is not logical."

"Forgive me. My logic falters where my son is concerned."

"Who then," called the High Priestess, gazing past Sarek, "is the keeper of thy son's Katra?"

"I am!" declared McCoy, stepping in front of the others.

The priestess's eyes grew cloudy as she sought the wisdom that lay deep within her. Again she spoke. "Thou must be warned. If we attempt Fal-Tor-Pan and fail, then all our powers cannot save thee. The dangers are thine; let the choice be thine."

Bones remained silent for a moment, but his companions could tell that he had made his decision even before it was asked of him. He swallowed hard and said, "I choose the danger."

"Come thou forward."

It was a simple ceremony and a gentle one. Gentle music, gentle chanting, and the gentle stirring of the wind through the temple chimes. Yet, as Jim and his friends stood there, an unseen energy seemed to swell up and fill the vast temple. It was like a kind of light that could not be seen, only felt.

As the hours wore on, the power of that "light" grew. It radiated outward from the temple to the mountainside and beyond, until lightning split the cloudless air.

The beauty, the power, the waiting were almost too much for the former crew of the *Enterprise*. Excited, hopeful, but also exhausted, they made their way out of the temple one by one and settled to the ground to rest. . . .

Daylight was just breaking when the High Priestess exited the temple on her throne, carried aloft on her monks, shoulders. All but one of them wore hooded robes of black. The outstanding one, a tall and slow-moving figure, was covered in shimmering white.

Jim leaped to his feet. "Spock!"

The figure slowed, stopped, and turned to face him. There was a look of wonderment in his eyes as he drew back his hood. He gazed at this strangely eager, almost trembling, man from Earth. "I know you . . . do I not?"

"Yes!"

Moments passed during which the new Spock groped to find the memories of the old one. Slowly, at first, images came to him: a battle in space; the radiation room of a ship; his own death.

"The crew?" he asked with concern. "The crew of the *Enterprise*?"

"You saved us, Spock! You saved us all! Don't you remember?"

Spock looked at him calmly, in the way of a Vulcan. "Jim," he said softly. "Your name is Jim."

"Yes!"

All at once, memories flooded his mind from all directions: memories of experiences shared together; memories of words spoken between them that were deeply felt.

He said them now, once again. "I have been . . . and ever shall be . . . your friend."

Jim wanted to throw his arms around Spock in a wild impulse! But he refrained; you didn't do that to a Vulcan. Still, he needed to embrace and share the joy of this moment with someone. He flung his arms around the weary, staggering McCoy. Then the whole crew rushed together, laughing, hugging, and crying all at the same time.

In that moment they all shared in a vision. It was of the great and noble starship *Enterprise*, their floating home and gallant companion in adventure for so many years. Born for the stars and deserving of her reputation as a starship par excellence, the *Enterprise*, like her fearless crew, would enjoy more than a small measure of immortality in the annals of space exploration and the human pursuit of intergalactic adventure.